DESIGN BY YVETTE LENHART

EGMONT
We bring stories to life

First published by Egmont USA, 2009
443 Park Avenue South, Suite 806
New York, NY 10016

Text copyright © 2009 Walter Dean Myers
Illustrations copyright © 2009 Christopher Myers
All rights reserved

10 9 8 7 6 5 4 3 2 1

www.egmontusa.com
www.walterdeanmyers.net

LIBRARY OF CONGRESS CATALOGING-IN-PUBLICATION DATA

Myers, Walter Dean, 1937 –
Looking like me / by Walter Dean Myers; illustrated by Christopher Myers.
p. cm.
Summary: Jeremy sets out to discover all of the different "people" that make him who he is,
including brother, son, writer, and runner.
ISBN 978-1-60684-001-6 (hardcover picture book) – ISBN 978-1-60684-041-2 (reinforced library
binding) [1. Individuality—Fiction. 2. Family life—New York (State)—Harlem—Fiction. 3. African
Americans—Fiction. 4. Harlem (New York, N.Y.)—Fiction.] I. Myers, Christopher, ill. II. Title.
PZ7.M992Loo 2009
[E]—dc22
2009014640

CPSIA tracking label information: Printed in Singapore by CS Graphics · Date of Production:
August 17, 2009 · Cohort: Batch 1

LOOKING LIKE ME

BY WALTER DEAN MYERS

ILLUSTRATED BY CHRISTOPHER MYERS

EGMONT

USA | New York

I LOOKED IN THE MIRROR

AND WHAT DID I SEE?

A REAL HANDSOME DUDE

LOOKING JUST LIKE ME.

ALONG CAME MY SISTER,

FINE AS SHE CAN BE.

"HEY, JEREMY," SHE SAID,

"YOU'RE LITTLE
BROTHER TO ME."

SHE PUT OUT HER FIST.

I GAVE IT A BAM!

JEREMY AND BROTHER, THAT'S WHO I AM.

ALONG CAME MY FATHER.

HE SAID, "HAVING FUN?

BECAUSE IF YOU ARE,

YOU NEED TO
ADD SON."

HE PUT OUT HIS FIST.

I GAVE IT A BAM!

I'M JEREMY, BROTHER, AND MY FATHER'S SON.

I GOT A
STRANGE
FEELING
I WASN'T
HALF DONE!

"AREN'T YOU A WRITER?"

ASKED MY TEACHER, MISS KAY.

"I SAW YOU WRITING IN YOUR BOOK TODAY."

"I'M A WRITER, SPINNING DRAMAS THAT DANCE ACROSS THE STAGE, A POET WEAVING MYSTERIES THAT LIVE UPON THE PAGE."

MISS KAY PUT OUT HER FIST.

I GAVE IT A BAM!

SAY JEREMY,
SAY BROTHER,
SAY SON,
SAY WRITER,
THAT'S WHO I AM.

I'M WALKING TALL AND I'M WALKING PROUD. LOOKED IN THE MIRROR—

I LOOK LIKE A CROWD.

"YOU'RE A CITY CHILD."

MY SKINNY MAILMAN GRINNED.

"AND I SEE YOU'RE REALLY LOVING THE CITY THAT YOU'RE IN."

"I'M A CITY CHILD. I LOVE THE DIZZY HEIGHTS, THE CONCRETE, THE STEEL, THE BRIGHT NEON LIGHTS."

THE MAILMAN
LIFTED HIS FIST.

I GAVE IT
A BAM !

IT IS KIND OF AMAZING
ALL THE PEOPLE I AM.

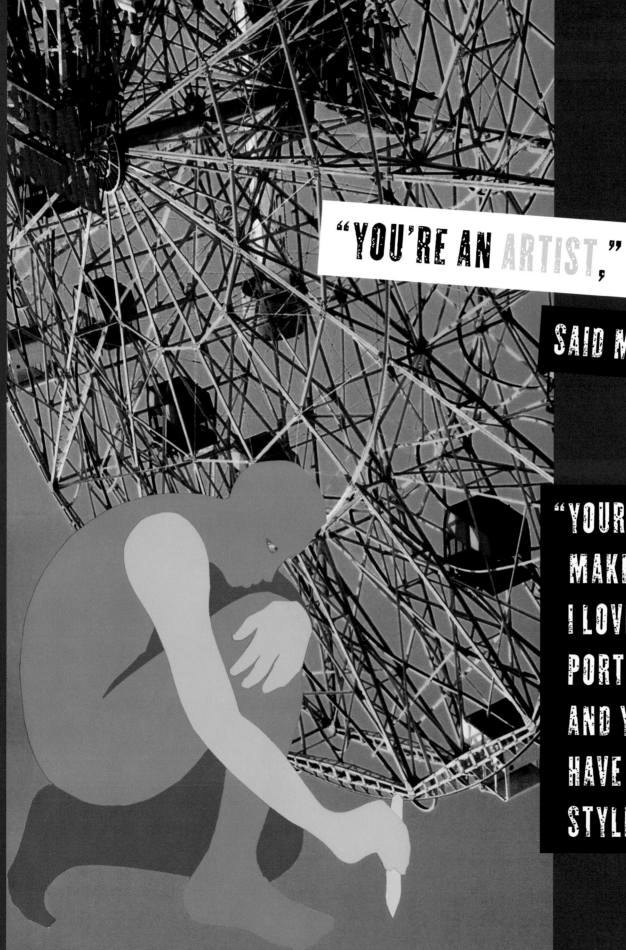

"YOU'RE AN ARTIST,"

SAID MY GRANDMA.

"YOUR PICTURES MAKE ME SMILE. I LOVE YOUR FUNNY PORTRAITS, AND YOUR SCENES HAVE SO MUCH STYLE!"

GRANDMA'S
RINGS AND
BANGLES
GAVE SUCH A
NOISY

BAM!

THEY WERE
REALLY
CELEBRATING
THE KIND
OF GUY I AM.

"I KNOW THAT YOU'RE A DANCER," SAID A SWEET GIRL WHIRLING BY.

"YOU MOVE YOUR FEET TO A SALSA BEAT

WITH A TWINKLE IN YOUR EYE."

SHE PUT OUT
HER FIST.

I GAVE
IT A
BAM!

I ADDED DANCER
TO THE ANSWER
OF JUST WHO I AM!

I KNOW THAT I'M A TALKER WITH MANY TALES TO TELL.

JOKES AND NEWS AND SECRETS — I HOPE I TELL THEM WELL.

MY WORDS ARE SOMETIMES HURRIED; AT TIMES THEY COME OUT SLOW.

AT TIMES THEY FLY LIKE SNOWFLAKES WITH EVERYWHERE TO GO.

SOMETIMES I
LET MY WORDS
GO FREE,
LIKE MARBLES
OFF A SHELF.

SOMETIMES I
GIVE MYSELF A
BAM
AND KEEP THEM
TO MYSELF.

I SAW KAREN RUNNING,
SO I RAN, TOO.
SHE SAID, "HEY, JEREMY.
WHAT'S UP WITH YOU?"

I SAID, "I'M A RUNNER.

I JUST LOVE TO RACE

WITH THE SPINNING EARTH

BENEATH ME, THE WIND

BLOWING IN MY FACE."

I GAVE IT A BAM!

WHEN SHE PUT OUT HER FIST.

THEN I ADDED RUNNER TO MY "I AM" LIST.

MY MOM CALLS
ME A DREAMER,

A SILVER-RAYED MOONBEAMER,

SPREADING FANTASIES ACROSS

THE HARLEM SKY.

I DREAM OF SECRET PLACES,

PLAID CLOUDS AND HIDDEN FACES,

BLACK KNIGHTS AND MAIDS

WHO SWOON AND SIGH.

MY MOM PUT OUT HER FIST.

I GAVE IT A GENTLE BAM,

BECAUSE THAT'S THE KIND OF

DREAMER THAT I AM.

WHY DON'T
YOU FIND
A MIRROR
AND SOME
FRIENDS
ALONG THE
WAY?

THINK OF
ALL THE
THINGS
YOU DO
AND ALL
THE THINGS
THEY SAY.

MAKE A
LONG LIST IF
YOU WANT
TO — HAVE
YOURSELF
AN "I AM"
JAM.

THEN GIVE
YOURSELF
A GREAT BIG
SMILE AND
YOUR FIST
A GREAT BIG

BAM!

We've looked in the mirror and what did we see? Two handsome dudes and a

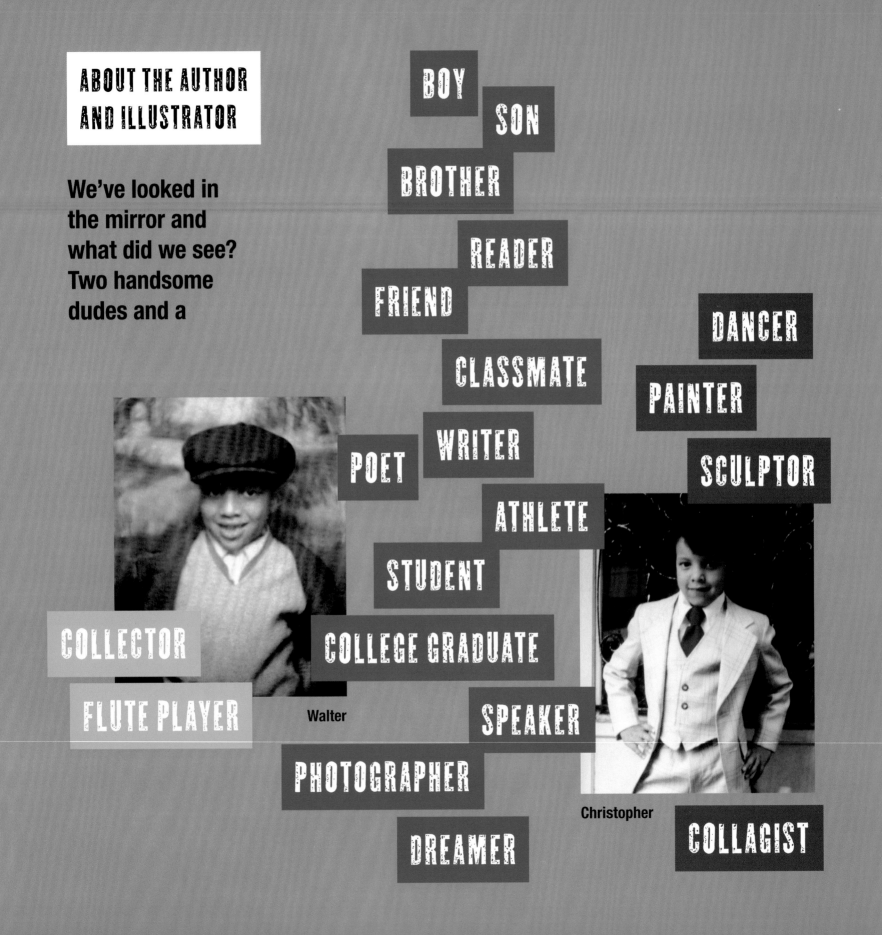

BOY

SON

BROTHER

READER

FRIEND

DANCER

CLASSMATE

PAINTER

WRITER

POET

SCULPTOR

ATHLETE

STUDENT

COLLECTOR

COLLEGE GRADUATE

FLUTE PLAYER

Walter

SPEAKER

PHOTOGRAPHER

Christopher

COLLAGIST

DREAMER